Winston
Won't Come Out

Written and Illustrated by
DIANE SIMPSON

Happy reading!
Diane Simpson

Chapters

Chapter 1
A Letter of Concern

Tom Tortoise shook his head in disbelief at Ruby Mouse's letter. "Dear Tom, please come quickly. Little Winston has gone into his shell and refuses to come out. He's not eating, and it has been several days. I am very worried."

Tom thought to himself, Ruby knows a tortoise doesn't do anything quickly. He wondered about Winston too. How unusual for Winston to not come out. The little turtle loved to swim, warm his face in the sun, and ate all day long. "I guess I'd best take the sailboat. It's quicker than me."

The wooden dock groaned under his feet. "A quiet sail south might be nice," he said, hoisting himself onto the boat. He reached for the handle on the floor and pulled the storage lid open. Three life jackets were tucked beside his lucky rubber duck. "All good," he thought to himself.

Scanning the shore he said, "Good news: looks like the frog next door, Damian, was still sleeping." Unfurling the white sails, a smile spread across his face. This trip was going to be peaceful, he thought, as he set sail into the wind.

Thud, thud. A frog landed on the dock.

A powerful feeling of dread came over Tom.

"Hey there! Say, where are you going? Early in the morning, isn't it? Did you hear about Winston?" Damian leapt onto the bow railing.

"I'm in a hurry Damian, no time to talk," Tom said, tossing the rope onto the deck. "See you when I get back."

"Ruby Mouse sent me a letter. Did you get a letter?" Leaping onto the port side of the boat, his green face turned upward, anticipating answers. When he received none, he continued. "Ruby said Winston won't come out, said I needed to come quickly. Can I come with you?"

Tom Tortoise had known Damian Lilypad all his life. The frog had a mud and grass home close to the water's edge. A few jumps onto the shore away was Tom's home, a tidy hut made of rocks with several rooms. Damian visited often. Tom had never met another creature that asked as many questions as Damian. The frog had an unending curiosity.

"Damian, you are already on my boat." Tom took a deep breath. "Listen, it's a long trip in a small sailboat, and I don't want to hurt your feelings but..."

"Wonderful! Then I can go too!"

Tom wanted to say no. However, watching Damian bouncing with delight across his deck, he could not. "Yes," he said despite his better judgement, "You can come. Please try to limit the questions. I run out of answers fast."

"Hey what's in there?" Damian said flipping open the storage lid. "Red floating jackets and oh look! What is this? A rubber duck?"

Lifting Damian out of the box Tom said, "Never mind, it's a storage box with emergency stuff."

"What's the duck for?" Damian said, lifting it into the air. The duck, close in size to Damian, had a wide smile and big eyes.

"No, leave it alone!" Shooting a glare at Damian, Tom said, "It's a good luck charm for the sailboat. Now put it back!" Snatching the duck and gently placing it into the box.

"Why so feisty?" said Damian.

"The duck is special, since it was the last gift Dad gave to me before, you know, he passed away. When I sail alone, it makes me feel as though Dad is still sailing with me."

"I'm sorry." Pouting and moving to the stern, Damian mumbled to himself. "How was I supposed to know? It looks like a toy, just a silly duck."

With Damian at the stern, Tom took advantage of the moment of quiet to think. His father taught him to sail, but understanding directions never stuck with him. If he sailed around the edge of the lake, he'd eventually reached his destination. This was a much easier solution. Crossing a huge expanse of Sparrow Lake, he would have to navigate in directions guided by the position of the sun. Heading west, east, north, and south looked the same from far out on the lake.

Damian snuck back to the center of the boat and hung onto the mast. "Seems like we are close to the shore still. Are you scared of the deep water?"

"I have my reasons," he said eyeing the curious frog. "Every good sailor knows how to avoid Big Tree Island. Now let me concentrate on the route." Raising his chin, he set his eyes on the shadows below the surface.

"What are you looking at? Is there treasure down there? Do you think there's mermaids?" said Damian.

"Dark shadows." Before Damian could ask, he said, "Are rocks that are near the surface, can damage the hull of the boat." Pointing at a grey rock's dark form, Tom said, "There, see it?"

Damian leaned over the rail to look, however, his bulging eyes showed Tom the little frog

was about to burst with curiosity. "In all my years I have never heard tell of treasure and I have never seen a mermaid."

"You know everything! I like that about you," said Damian. "Too bad about the mermaids. Winston might come out to see a mermaid."

"I think we all would," said Tom laughing.

The sailboat split the water, leaving a trail of ripples sparkling from the midday sun. With the warmth of the rays on his face, Tom tried to recall his father's lessons. The sails, the helm, the knots, all lessons he recalled were set in his mind. Except, south, north, west, and east, became a blur of mixed-up images.

Shaking his head, he said to himself, "Back in the day, I wasn't good at listening and now here I am, not good at remembering." Luckily, Damian hadn't noticed.

A soft melody drifting on the wind broke Tom out of his reflections.

"Say! You hear music? Tom! Do you hear it?"

"Yes, I do. Must be the racoons." An idea occurred to him, and giddiness swelled in his chest. I can convince Damian to travel with the racoons and have a quiet sail to myself.

"The racoons are fun. We should stop over, it'd be nice to take a break. Don't you agree?" said Damian.

"I guess so." Good, thought Tom, they'd be at the inlet soon and Damian would be off his boat. His idea made him grin, and he thought, I can sail in total peace and quiet. "It's going to get tricky here, no distractions please."

"I can help. Look out little fish!" Stradling the ledge and dangling his head over said, "Hey, how do you steer?"

Tom gave him a sideways smirk. "The helm controls the rudder." Tom, squeezing his eyes shut, tried to dig up more patience.

"I'm doing it again, aren't I?" Pouting, Damian said, "And you've run out of answers already."

"Damian, you are just being yourself, a curious little frog."

His face brightened. "Ha, you don't fool me, I bet you have a lot more answers. You're smart. I want to be as smart as you Tom."

"Thanks," said Tom pleased with the flattery. "Now look ahead, that's where the music is coming from."

Tom, muttering to himself said, "He is inquisitive, be nice to him." Yet, he couldn't help imagining being on the boat alone. Tranquil solitude and the wind cooling his face. If he could convince Damian to travel with the racoons, he'd gain back his tranquility. He stared into the water at his reflection and in his heart, felt hope. Nobody's going to figure out I don't know everything about sailing.

Chapter 2
Hard to Say No

The music grew louder. "The racoons live around the far side of that inlet," Tom said. "We can stop for a quick visit, but I must insist we stay just for a few minutes. Ruby is waiting for our help."

A land mass curved like a giant banana from the shore and out into the lake. In the distance a wooden hut sat in the shadows amongst the trees. Rusted red, the tin roof stood out amongst the greenery. A deep vibrating hum arose from a wooden instrument. Vox, a large puffy racoon, plucked the strings with her claws while Leo, a much smaller racoon, sang. Noticing Tom's boat approaching, the racoons went quiet, and the music stopped. Vox and Leo's faces lit up with excitement. Recognizing the boat and their friends on board, the racoons began waving. "Hello! Hello there!" They ran towards the beach to greet them.

The sailboat made a soft squish into the sandy shore. Tom clambered over the boat wall, slid down the rope, and landed knee deep into the water. Damian splashed down beside him, swam ahead, and stood on the sand surveying the racoons.

"Hello Tom, hello Damian," said Leo, the smallest of the raccoons. "Your sailboat is here just in time. We have finished practicing and are ready to travel."

"Hello," Damian said looking from one racoon to the other. "Where did you get a

wheelbarrow? Are you going to see Winston too? Where did that..."

Tom held his hand in the air to silence him and said, "Enough with the questions please." Behind the racoons sat an overloaded wheelbarrow stuffed boxes and bags of snacks. Resting against a tree were several types of instruments. "I see you've been busy preparing."

"Our wheelbarrow has a flat tire and we've no time to visit the dump to find another one," said Vox trying to push the wheelbarrow and squishing the tire into the ground.

With sorrowful eyes, Leo said, "You see, flat as a pancake and we must help little Winston."

"Of course, we are all concerned," Tom said. His mood turned gloomy. There'll be no escaping Damian and all the questions now, he thought to himself. Since the racoons were unable to travel on land, he had a hunch about what Vox and Leo would suggest.

"What's a dump? It sounds fun. Say, can you..." Damian stopped talking, noticing Tom's stare.

"Your sailboat is lovely and looks like there is lots of room for snacks," said Leo. "Excellent timing, showing up just when we needed a lift."

"I like snacks. Do you have a bag of flies?" Damian said, digging through the wheelbarrow's supplies.

Shaking his head and stopping Vox from attempting to reply to the frog, he said, "I am sorry, but I can't." The two frowning racoons cast their gaze at the ship and back to Tom. "It's not meant for so many passengers. I mean, I'd like you to join us. It's just not safe."

His boat had become noisy enough with the little frog. Adding singing racoons would be the last thing he needed.

"They have cookies!" said Damian holding up the box. "Winston loves cookies. You must let them come now."

Leo held up a letter stained with greasy fingerprints. "But Ruby Mouse asked us to come quickly." The racoons held it out to show Tom and Damian. "Please, we can show Winston how to play the cello, and the trumpet, and the drums." Behind them stood an assortment of instruments resting against a tree.

Concerned about his poor sense of direction, Tom sulked, he could see no way out of this problem. Beside him the racoons stood grinning with hope.

"There is increased risk." Tom said. "I haven't enough room in the cabin, not enough life jackets, and the instruments are too heavy for my boat."

"We are great at solving problems," said Leo and his eyes narrowed and he nodded at Vox. The racoons began whispering with tails twitching. Leo, explaining his ideas, threw waving hands in the air.

Watching the racoons chatter Tom said, "There is no possible way to make this work and I will have to refuse in a friendly way."

Damian chuckled. "You aren't good at saying no. Besides, I hope they get to come with us. I have more questions for them."

"I bet you do."

Tom knew Damian had a point; he did have a tough time saying no. It'd be best to leave now, and he could just say goodbye. Turning, he began walking towards the boat when a light tap on his shell made him pause.

Vox put her hands on her hips and said, "We have decided. Although, I think my idea is just as good." She stuck her tongue out at her brother. "Once again, we will use Leo's plan."

Tom, jiggling his finger in the air, said, "Time is wasting. I have no choice but to set sail now." Turning, he made his way down to the beach with Damian leaping alongside him. Behind him he heard footsteps in the sand and grunting.

"Wait, we have a brilliant solution, mostly my idea, but Vox did have a few points," said Leo. Vox rolled her eyes. "It's very simple really." Standing on the edge of the shore each raccoon held an instrument for Tom to inspect.

"Alright, tell me," Tom said.

"A trumpet for me and a cello for Vox," said Leo. "You can hear it everywhere." Vox plucked the strings of the cello sending deep thrums echoing across the lake. "Isn't it wonderful!"

"What do you think Tom?" said Damian. "Can they come too?"

Tom pinched his lips together. "Uhm, well..." Unhappy about the instruments, he had to decide which problem was worse, refusing Vox and Leo or sailing with Vox and Leo. Looking at the racoons' eager faces he thought to himself, they are worried about Winston too. He let out a long deep sigh, deciding to suffer with the noise. "Yes, you may come aboard."

"Oh Tom, thank you!" said Vox hugging him. "We will sing songs all the way there to make the trip merry!"

"Great," he said, attempting to smile, more noise. With a shove from the oars, he set the boat drifting into the lake.

Chapter 3
Into the Deep

Tom noticed Damian questioning the raccoons about the instruments. Vox and Leo responded with their hands flailing with explanations. Perhaps the racoons will be a desirable distraction for Damian, Tom thought.

With the added weight, the boat needed the deeper waters at the center of the lake. His grip tightening on the helm, he said to himself, "It'll be okay. My friends will be okay." The wind caught the sails increasing their speed. His eyes stared into the depths scanning for dangers. Glancing at the sun he made a wish, please don't let them discover I don't know directions. He'd steer straight and that might work.

"How much further? Did you know racoons are excellent swimmers? Do you want a cookie?" said Damian.

"I see you managed to bring snacks on board." Tom took the cookie and bit into it. "We must pass Big Tree Rock as the half-way mark. I am glad to hear they swim."

Deep water hid its dangers. Tom dared not take his eyes away. The frog kept talking, kept distracting him.

"One more question."

"If you must. I mean, go ahead." Tom kept his gaze on the water.

"Aren't you afraid of the eagle on Big Tree Rock?"

Lifting his gaze and turning towards Damian, he said, "Afraid?" Looking at the raccoons he saw their eyes were wild with fear. Damian bit his lower lip.

"Tell us Tom, is the eagle dangerous?" said Vox with quivering whiskers. "We've heard scary stories."

He remembered an encounter. Many years ago, on a sailing trip with his father, a shift in the wind brought them too close to the island. The immense eagle dove into the water and rose with a wiggling fish in its sharp talons. With powerful beats of its wings the giant bird disappeared into its nest with the meal. His father warned him, stay away from the eagle and her island if you don't want to become lunch.

"I have come closer than I care to admit." Tom wanted to reassure his passengers, yet, he had to tell the truth. Tom sucked in a big breath. "Yes, we all should be afraid of the eagle."

Chapter 4
Be Afraid

He'd heard the same song three times, and it grew louder with each rendition. The song started again. Having learned the words, Damian joined in. Tom had memorized it too but refused to sing. Cello strings thrummed and and noisy singing rattled his brain. Enough with the noise, he thought to himself. They began again.

In the water, with a fish so blue,

We swim together, me and you.

Gentle waves, with joyful spins,

Fins and scales, a dance begins.

Through the sea, we play and glide,

Adventure deep, side by side.

He missed the sound he could no longer hear; the water slapping against the hull of the sailboat. The sooner they reached the south shore the better.

"We are half-way there!" Tom said thinking this good news would distract them.

Leo, sitting on Vox's shoulders said, "I see Big Tree Rock!" Her black fingers pointing in the distance to a rocky mound with a single tree pushing into the sky.

Damian had climbed to the top of the sail. His green body stood out against its whiteness.

"The other frogs told me stories," he said sliding down the roof of the cabin. "The island doesn't like visitors."

"Islands don't have feelings," Tom said frowning. "You are talking nonsense. It's just a big rock with a big tree." He nodded to the racoons. "Nothing to worry about," he said to comfort his friends.

His Father had fought the strong wind. The current swept around the far side, and somehow, they managed to steer the boat into safer waters. Stay clear, he'd said to Tom with a finger pointing at the forbidden island. This lesson, he never forgot.

Damian, looking grim said, "Sure, but we are concerned. You know, about the eagle, who lives on the rock." Balancing himself on the ledge he surveyed the island.

Squinting at the sun, Tom thought, "I can't find the south until the sun starts to sink in the west." He guessed at his direction. "We are going south, past the rock. Now get back to the deck before you tumble overboard."

"What do eagles eat? How big are they? Have you seen the eagle?"

Vox said, "I believe we are heading more south-west with a bit more west than south."

"They eat frogs, eat racoons, eat tortoises," said Leo. "Vox is right, heading south is taking us closer to the island, which means we are moving west south."

"Enough!" said Tom. "We are going to sail right past it." He felt the direction of the wind and stared at the position of the sun. "Yes, right past, just like I said."

Moments later Big Tree Rock appeared closer. In the center of the island stood a tree with a head of green leaves spreading like an umbrella against the sky. A large nest sat on top like a crown of twigs.

"Oh no!" said Tom. Waves clawing at the boat were pushing it towards the island. "The current is too strong." He ran to the ropes. "Vox, Leo, Damian, help me turn the sails!" Returning to the helm, it took all his strength to stay upright. He knew his boat proved no match for the current.

"What do we do?" said Vox.

"Prepare for the worst," he said. Lifting the storage lid, Tom began handing life jackets to the racoons. Struggling to stay upright they fastened the straps. Then he sized up Damian and realized a problem.

"I don't have a small enough safety-vest for you," Tom said. "But I do have this." He handed the rubber duck to Damian. "It floats upright." Pausing, Tom added, "My father gave me the duck many years ago. It was the last trip he sailed with me. It's special, but so are you. Take good care of duck."

"Now lucky duck can keep me safe," Damian said climbing on its back. Wrapping his skinny frog arms around its neck he said, "I will take good care of your lucky-daddy's-ducky." The pads on his fingers stuck to the soft rubber. "This is going to work great."

"I agree and just call it a duck." Tom gave him a smile and hoped he didn't look worried. "Stay here," he said. Returning to the bow, he strapped his own life jacket on and studied

his course, determined to steer the sailboat between the rocks. Gripping the helm, his arms straining to keep it steady. He knew this wasn't going to be easy.

"Let me help you," said Vox wrapping her hands below Tom's on the helm. Behind them Leo clung to Damian and watched the island growing nearer.

"Winston will have to wait longer for our help," said Vox. Tom's head dropped and he let out a groan. "It's okay Tom, this isn't your fault the current is so strong. Besides, your friends are here to help you."

True, Tom thought. "Thank-you Vox. I'm glad you are here."

Leo shouted over the waves, "We are the ones that need help now!"

Chapter 5
Missing

Despite their grip on the helm, the sailboat aimed towards the island. Scanning between the waves, Tom did his best to steer towards a gap between the rocks.

"Everyone, hold onto something. We are going to hit the beach hard," Tom said.

Thud, crunch, thud.

Tom, landing on his belly, flung out his hand to catch Vox as she spun past him. Her body crashed into the side wall. Leo, rolling across the deck, smashed into her, forming a jumble of furry limbs. The ship had come to a complete stop.

"That was lucky. The boat found a sandy spot and missed the rocks," said Vox leaning over the edge.

Standing, Tom spun his head around. "Where is Damian?" The yellow rubber duck was missing too, he shouted again. "Damian? Where are you?"

No response.

"Everyone, look for Damian." Tom stepped onto the large rock next to his boat. His keen eyes skimmed the frothing waves and the sandy shore. Where could he have gone? The raccoons stood on the beach looking out at the water.

"Damian! Answer me!" said Tom.

"The yellow duck is not here either," said Vox. "Could he be out on the lake?" she said casting her eyes out into the waves.

"No, he has to be close by," he said not seeing the frog or the duck.

"Tom," said Leo, "He can swim. He will be all right."

"The duck is lucky, remember?" Vox gave him a weak smile.

"It's my fault," Tom held his head in his hands. "Too many passengers on the boat. I should have said no. A good sailor would have said no."

"You sail well and I'm glad you said yes to us Tom," said Leo. "We'd have no other way of getting to Winston."

"Might have been better off with a broken wheelbarrow."

"Nonsense," said Vox. "We will find him together and get off this dreadful island."

Cool sand made his feet feel heavy. Taking a few steps, he'd stop, turn towards the lake, and call out. "Damian! Can you hear me! Damian where are you?" Squinting, Tom tried to see the rubber duck. It should be easy to see, he thought.

The sand around his feet turned dark grey. A shadow he recognized surrounded him. Tilting his head to the sky he saw it. The eagle, circling above.

"Screech! Screech!" The eagle, soaring lower with every pass, had her cold stare locked on them.

Chapter 6
A Matter of Hats

"The eagle, it's the eagle!" said Tom. The yellow beak, attached to a bright white head was unmistakable against the blue sky. "Run, to that opening in the rocks!"

A pile of rocks, surrounding a small cave, offered enough space for the fleeing friends to squeeze inside. The eagle landed with a flurry of feathers flapping. Tom could see her sharp taloned feet and powerful feathered legs through the opening.

"Leave us alone," he said in his bravest voice.

"Alone? What do you know about being alone." The large bird had an awful squawking voice. The white head tipped sideways and yellow eyes peered at them. "Who are you? Come out so I can see you better."

"I am Tom Tortoise and these are my friends, Vox and Leo Racoon. We aren't staying."

"What a shame, I do enjoy having company." Her tone almost sounded sincere with a hint of sorrow. "I am always alone on this rock."

The racoons, hugging each other, were looking at Tom. He wondered, if Damian were here, what would he ask?

"Is this a trick? How can we be sure you won't eat us?" Tom said.

The eagle chuckling said, "I eat fish. You are not a fish. That means I won't eat you. See? It's that simple. Now step out and let me look at you." The eagle's head twisted side to side with curious eyes watching them. "Please," she said.

The racoons were cowering with whiskers twitching. He said, "A bald eagle, like you, could fly anywhere to have company."

The eagle let out an earsplitting cry. "Bald! Don't call me bald! You are cruel like everyone else!" Shaking her wings in distress she said, "oh, my feelings ache. I am wounded."

Tom's mouth dropped open, had no reply. He had hurt the eagle's feelings. However, he had no idea what to say next.

"Now you did it! She's going to eat us for sure!" said Leo.

"I'm sorry. I didn't mean to injure your feelings. Truly, we are sorry," said Tom. "I didn't know bald is a sensitive subject," he whispered to Vox and Leo.

The squawking voice stopped crying and said, "This is why I can't have any friends. Everyone that comes here..." she wiped tears from her eyes, "reminds me that I am bald. Why must they tell me? Do they think I don't know?"

"We won't mention it again," said Leo. "We racoons are happy to keep you company." An awkward pause followed while the eagle sniffled. "If all you eat is fish, just fish and nothing but fish, I suppose we can come out and meet you."

"I also enjoy crackers." Clearing her throat with an "Eh-hem" she said, "I assure you; my diet is picky."

Tom said, "I will come out, just me."

"We will hang onto your legs in case we need to save you," said Leo. The racoons held onto Tom's feet, ready to tug him back under the ledge. Tom took two large steps into the sunshine

and tilted his head to see the large bird looming over him. On top of the great bird's head sat a brown hat adorned with flowers.

"My apologies for our previous behavior," Tom said, "What a lovely hat." The eagle's wing tapped the hat, pleased at the compliment. "This is my first time meeting an eagle up close." The eagle's feathers were the pure white of new snow. "You can call me Tom. Nice to meet you."

Extending her wing she shook his hand. Beaming with a wide smile she said, "Call me Bertie."

Tom introduced the racoons and Bertie seemed pleased to meet them all. However, he decided not to mention Damian. The frog would be all on his own against the big eagle. Vox explained to Bertie their worry for their friend Winston and their mission to help the little turtle.

Bertie listened closely. "Hmm, a turtle inside his shell and refusing to come out? Any idea why?"

Tom shrugged, "Ruby Mouse has tried her best to coax him out. Nothing has worked. Which is why we are in a hurry."

"I've never heard such an interesting predicament." Bertie said. "You can hurry later. Let's have snacks." She began walking along the tumbled rocks. "Follow me, I have a hut not far away."

Tom held up his hand to protest and whispered to the racoons. "I don't trust her. I say we find the frog and leave."

"I could use a snack," said Vox, and began toddling over the rocks following Bertie.

"Vox, wait," said Leo wrapping his hands around her striped tail. "It's not a good idea."

Planting his heels into the ground, Leo's body dragged behind Vox. "You have to stop; we have to discuss a plan!"

Vox pausing, raised her eyebrows at her smaller brother. "Leo, you always make the plans. It's my turn." Yanking her tail out of Leo's hands she said, "If I choose a bad idea, oh well at least it's my idea for once! Besides, I'm hungry and she has snacks."

"Please stop!" said Leo but Vox was already taking large steps over the rocks towards Bertie.

Chapter 7
A Trap?

Leo, watching Vox totter after the eagle said, "I thought she liked my plans." He spun towards Tom. "Now what do we do?"

"Don't worry Leo, she likes your plans. Vox is hungry. Nobody makes sense when they are hungry." Tom shook his head. "Let's fetch Vox, find Damian, and get back to the boat as quickly as possible."

"Agreed," said Leo, "No more wasting time."

Following Bertie, they clambered over rocks to the far side of the island. Grass grew in patches between the rugged boulders. They arrived at a hut with a door, four walls, and a roof made of entwined twigs.

"I like to make forts in my spare time. Most fall apart, but this one is my best." Bertie smiled and held the door open. On her head, the hat's brim flopped in the wind. "Please come inside," Bertie waved her wing in a grand gesture. "Have a snack, have a rest, have a chat."

"How generous of you, but no thank you," said Tom, his heart pounding in his chest. He'd never defied anyone before. Saying no felt right, yet it wasn't easy to say.

Bertie's eyes held a desperate plea for them to enter, begging them to fall into her trap. Tom's eyes narrowed, "I have a perfectly good shell and don't need a hut." Her smile made

him nervous. "Besides, we can't stay."

Vox rubbing her hands together said, "Do I smell raspberries?"

Bertie laughed, "Oh yes, oh yes. I have cheese, crackers, and raspberries."

Vox's lips were quivering. "Alright, I think I might have a taste." She strutted inside inhaling the delicious smells. "Oh my, look at all the food!"

Swiveling his head from Leo to Vox, Tom said, "We don't have time for this." He threw his arms into the air. "Ruby is waiting for us to help Winston come out!"

"I know. First, we must drag Vox out." Rolling his eyes, Leo stepped into the hut. "Come on, we can't let her eat everything."

Hesitating, Tom sized up Bertie. She smiled but the eyes held the cold stare of a bird of prey. Stepping inside the hut he had a terrible feeling in his gut.

A round wooden table sat in the middle of the hut. Boxes of crackers, cookies and fruits Tom had never seen before piled on top. He reached for blueberries from a bright green basket. How did Bertie get all this food, he wondered.

Strange hats hung from all four walls. "An impressive assortment," Tom said recognizing a white puffy chef's cap, a cowboy's brown curved brim, and a dark blue captain's hat. The collection extended across the roof.

"Everyone must wear a hat!" said Bertie. Before they could stop her, a ballcap landed on Vox, a pink baby bonnet on Leo, and a straw hat on Tom. She turned to survey them. "Much better." She reached for a case on the floor. "Orange Pop?" Opening pop cans with her talons, she placed one in front of each of her guests. "It's tasty, try it."

The guests hesitated; unsure what orange pop was.

Her eyes narrowed, "I said, try it!"

Wary of her temper, they took a sip.

"Uhm…this food, these hats," said Leo "Where do you get all of this?"

Waving her wing in the air Bertie said, "well, the people at the market love me! I take whatever I want." Slurping a gulp of orange pop, she let out a loud burp. "Like these hats. The people scream, they are so excited, and take pictures. Click, click, click," she said posing. "Then I fly away."

"Screaming hey? Do you think they might fear you?" said Tom. He tried the orange pop, coughed, and pushed the can away.

"Well, I am terrifying, but in a charming way," said Bertie.

Leaning towards the racoons' ears, Tom whispered, "we need an escape plan. Stall until you see a way out of here."

Vox and Leo asked about the market and the people. Bertie bragged about her market adventures. She described her favourite outdoor café where she found the best hats. The stories came one after another. Tom and his friends kept eating. It wasn't long before they'd had enough of Bertie and enough of her food.

"Thank you for the wonderful market stories," Tom said pausing to swallow a blueberry, "and of course, the snacks. You are a good host, but we need to be going. Winston, you recall, needs us." Tom stood and heading towards the door said, "We will certainly visit you again soon."

"Leave! On no, I will get more snacks, more stories." Berties eyes spread wide with alarm. "You must stay."

Vox took her hat off and hung it on the wall. "Thank-you, but like Tom said, Winston needs…"

"What?" A yellow talon foot stomped on the table, squishing a pop can. Bouncing food fell onto the floor. "I forbid it!" In one leap she shielded the door with her body. "Nobody is going anywhere!"

Chapter 8
Be My Guest

The terrible feeling in Tom's gut returned, clear now on why the island didn't have any visitors. Bertie had tricked them with food and lulled them to think nothing bad would happen.

Leo threw off his hat. "You can't keep us prisoner here!"

"You are guests," said Bertie, "My guests aren't allowed to leave." Her wings spread wide blocking the exit. "Now sit and listen to my stories."

Vox approached Bertie and said, "That's not how it works. Guests leave. Then they come back."

"I make the rules on this island." Her cackling voice hit a high shrill. Bertie's eyes narrowed "You are mine now, my guests stay."

The friends clung together behind the table. Orange pop dripping off its edge pooled at their feet. Berties body filled the doorway, blocking any chance of exiting the hut.

Tom stood with his back towards his friends, blocking them from Bertie. He whispered, "Vox, Leo, any ideas?"

"Just one and you won't like it," Vox said and whispered in his ear, "if we aren't nice, she won't want us here."

Oh no, thought Tom, this is a terrible idea! "Vox, shh! Don't' say anything."

"Do all eagles wear hats?" said Vox.

Leo joined in. "What about crows? Oh wait, they aren't bald, no they like shiny things."

The yellow beak dropping open, squeaked. "Crows? What do you mean?"

"Maybe, you should dye your white feathers black, look like a crow?" said Vox. "Nobody would call a crow bald. I'm sure the people at the market have dye for feathers."

"Stop it, there has to be another way," said Tom under his breath to Vox. Tom noticed Bertie's eyes starting to water around the rims. Her feathers began to quiver. "They don't mean it," said Tom. "We really liked your snacks and your hats. However, we need to be on our way."

"Why don't you have bald eagle friends? Be bald together?" said Vox.

Bertie's beak hung open, unable to answer the question.

Stepping between the racoons and Bertie, Tom said, "you are supposed to be bald, Bertie. There's no need for hats." Tears were rolling down her feathered cheeks. Torn between their need to escape and not wanting to hurt her feelings, Tom looked at the racoons and then at Bertie.

"Stop it!" said Bertie. "I'm not like other birds" Bertie crumbled to the floor crying. "I don't like being bald, and alone, and I don't understand how to make friends." Tugging the hat tighter over her head she said, "it's because I am bald. Nobody likes me."

"I can think of a few more reasons," said Leo. He held up his hands, about to count the reasons out on each finger.

"Enough!" said Tom frowning at the racoons. "Being mean isn't the answer to our problem."

Covering her face with her wings, loud sobs made Berties feathers shake. Tom patted her

wing. "You aren't bald. The feathers on your head are white and quite striking," said Tom. "It's okay if you like hats. We had fun wearing them too."

Bertie sniffed. "What?"

"Honest," Tom dared to say more. "Against a blue sky, your white feathered head is beautiful."

"This is a prank!" Peeking between the feathers of her wing she surveyed her guests.

They all shook their heads. "Not at all. I am being truthful." Tom surveyed the racoons with a warning look. "My friends here, were rude because they were scared."

"It's true, you are big and fierce," said Leo, "and the white brings out your yellow eyes." The raccoons, grinning, nodded in agreement. "We can teach you how to be friends. Sharing your hats and your snacks is a good start."

"How very sweet of you," Bertie said wiping her tears away. Her head bent sideways, listening. "Do you hear that? Somebody is making a noise." Her head twisted sideways concentrating on the sound.

"Squeak, squeak, squeak."

Bertie stuck her head out the door. "Such a strange noise."

Tom gasped. "I know that sound! It's lucky ducky."

"Squeak, squeak. Say, where are you guys? Why did you leave the boat? Is this a game of hide and seek?"

Tom, Vox, and Leo said his name together. "Damian!"

Chapter 9
Going This Way

Jumping up from the floor Bertie's face brightened. "Another guest! I will be right back." She rushed out, slamming the door behind her.

The guests heard something heavy sliding along the ground. Then, flapping wings were beating in the air.

Squeak. Squeak. "Oh no! Damian has no idea!" said Vox.

Tom pushed against the door. "Bertie put something heavy in the way to keep us inside."

"Guests are not prisoners!" said Tom, banging on the door. "Now is our chance. Leo, we need your ideas."

"Maybe Vox should give us an idea," he said crossing his arms over his chest. "She had the notion to follow Bertie into the hut. She can find us a way out."

Vox sighed. "It just happens that I do have an idea. Watch what fingers can do." Wiggling the branches loose, her fingers untied ropes. Leo decided to help and soon light shone through cracks. "Almost done," said Leo, continuing to unravel the wall. "Give it a push, Tom. The wall is all loosened."

Digging in his heels, Tom sent the wall crashing to the ground. Swirling wind rushed into the hut rocking the hats off their hooks and sending them soaring sky-high.

"Oh no, now we've really done it," said Leo.

Tom motioned to the shore. "Hurry, we don't want to explain this to Bertie." Over boulders they scrambled trying to rush. The boat seemed farther away than they recalled. In the distance Tom could see the white sail flapping in the wind.

Squeak, squeak. A sound echoed from below. "Why do you live on the island? Can you swim? Have you seen my friends?"

"Look! On the rocks," Tom said. "Bertie is hovering over something yellow. Hey, up here Damian!" A sense of relief swept over him for a moment, then a swell of fear.

Bertie had her head low over a crevice between the rocks. A bright yellow duck had become wedged into the crack. Damian sat on top of the rock watching her attempt to free the duck. "Come on, we have to save Damian," said Tom, "and get away from Bertie."

A feathered cap plopped into the water next to Bertie. Damian pointed at it. "Hey, is that one of your hats? Why is it in the water? Look, more hats are coming!" The breeze played with the hats like kites, spinning them up and out over the lake.

Twisting her white head towards the sky she let out a scream. "My hats! No, no, no!"

Damian shouted, "Tom, I'm over here!" Then he looked at Bertie. "I can swim fast. I will fetch what I can."

A blue ball cap spun on the surface, darkening with the absorbed water, and sinking out of sight. A chef's hat bobbed, a baby bonnet, and a red beret. Damian dove and set the soggy hats on the shore.

Tugging the duck free from the rocks, she said, "Ducky is rescued." Spreading her powerful wings and gliding along the surface, Bertie tried to rescue her beloved hats. Once her claws were full, she flew towards the big tree.

"Now's our chance. Let's get out of here," said Tom. "Damian, head to the boat."

Pressing his back against the rocks, Tom planted his feet on the hull. "We just need a little shove." Grunting, he forced the hull towards the lake. Rushing water surrounded the hull of the boat. Relieved, Tom splashed through the water towards the racoons. "Everyone, get on board."

Damian jumped onboard first. Tom and the raccoons clambering on next. For now, the waves had softened into gentle rolls, but soon the breeze would whip around the island. "Help me turn the sails. We need to catch the breeze and get away from Bertie."

"Why, what's wrong with Bertie? She saved my duck." Confused, Damian said, "did you know she doesn't have friends? Can we go back and try her snacks?"

"No!" said Tom, Leo, and Vox together.

Damian stumbling backwards, stood gawking at their faces. "Why, what happened, don't you like her?"

Tom didn't have time to explain. "Bertie is rather busy right now."

"She said south is that way," Damian said pointing out towards trees in the distance. "She said Winston is lucky to have so many friends."

The racoons nervously grinned at each other. Twisting their hands, they kept glancing over at Tom.

"Well, I'm going this way to go south," said Tom scanning the tree line in the distance. "The sun is over there, and we are going over here." He pointed to make sure they believed him. "South is this way."

Chapter 10
Somewhat South

Gaining speed, the sailboat cut through the water. Tom searched for any danger below the surface. He'd lost a lot of time and was determined to get it back. His passengers were thankfully huddling together and not questioning his sense of direction.

"I told Bertie that friends help each other. Then I fished out some of her hats. She asked me what we needed help with. I told her, we are eager to go south." Damian pointed towards the shore with tall pine trees. "South, she said, is that way."

In the distance they could see Bertie swooping into the lake and scooping up her hats. For a moment Tom felt sad for her, all alone on Big Tree Rock. Then again, relief swept over him to be away from her too.

"Bye Bertie! I hope you save every one of your hats!" Damian said, waving from the top of the cabin.

"Stop Damian, we are escaping from Bertie." Tom explained how they were tricked and needed to flee Big Tree Rock. "You see, and now we must hurry to Winston. Because of Bertie, we lost a lot of time."

Upset, Damian said, "Too bad. I found her nice." He kept his gaze towards the sky. Patting duck on the head he said, "can you sail faster than an eagle?" A shadow of broad wings flew

over the boat. Damian shouted, "Look, Bertie is coming too."

"You are going the wrong way!" Bertie said. "Follow me. Turn your sailboat." She circled around the boat with a blue hat in her clutches. "Let me help you. We can be friends."

Tom shook his head no.

"Why don't you trust her?" said Damian waving at her again. "Hi Bertie."

Tom let out sigh and said, "I explained why Damian." Ignoring her, Tom kept his eyes set on the shore, steering the sailboat into his chosen course.

"Hello Damian," said Bertie. "Please ask your friends to give me another chance." Bertie swooping low said, "I want to help you sail towards Winston."

Leo and Vox were whispering and planning. Leo stood in front of the helm and nudged Vox to speak. "Tom, she can help us get to Winston faster," she said, "save us time too." The racoons gave him encouraging grins.

Leo's finger pointed at Bertie, "trust her Tom. She doesn't understand how to make friends, but she does know how to get us to the right south."

"Well," said Tom watching Bertie circling above. He felt uneasy. He wanted to say no, and keep his friends protected, but what if the racoons were right? Bertie's smile did appear genuine. "Okay, we will follow."

Taking them in a new direction, Tom turned the sails to follow a happy Bertie. She coasted in front of the sailboat.

Behind him, Tom noticed the racoons whispering. It was obvious now; he had gone the wrong direction. "Alright you two, what is it?"

Leo spoke first, "it seems Bertie's south is different from your south. Which brings a question to mind."

"Are there two souths?" said Damian. "Like a south that is further away and a south that is closer?"

"No," said Tom. He was nervous to admit his faults. Three passengers stared at him. "I suppose you've noticed, so I should confess." Pausing, he tried to find the right words. "I didn't want passengers because you might figure out why I sail around the edge of the lake until I get where I am going." He shrugged, "tortoises are knowledgeable in many things. However, I have yet to learn directions. I'm not as smart as you think I am, Damian."

"Why don't you ask questions, somebody has to know how to do it," said Damian. "You are still the smartest animal on Sparrow Lake!"

Vox nodded in agreement. "Not to worry my friend. We've noticed you get lost often."

"Fortunately for you," said Leo, "I've come up with a plan."

"I think you intended to say, both of us have come up with a plan." Her eyes gazed upwards towards the eagle soaring above them. "It's flying right over us."

Bertie overheard the conversation from above and said, "I can teach you directions using the winds, the stars, and the sun."

"I would really like to learn," said Tom. Perhaps sailing to Big Tree Island, Tom thought, had been a lucky accident. A sense of delight bubbled up in his chest. He'd made a new friend and he'd learn directions!

Following Bertie, they soon found themselves approaching the southern shore. The sailboat slid onto the sandy beach and came to a gentle stop.

Ruby's house stood in a patch of grass next to a large fallen log. Extending across the beach, the log stretched out to the edge of Sparrow Lake. A sign hung on its door, "Winston's Log." Winston typically sat on top of the log sunning himself. Not today.

Chapter 11
Secrets in the Dark

"There he is," Tom said to his three passengers.

Ruby Mouse, looking concerned, stood on the top of the log gazing downward at the little red shell. "Ruby, hello!" The mouse's eyes brightened at the sight of them.

Holding the instruments above their heads, the raccoons wobbled across the sandy beach. Close behind them, Damian leapt towards Winston. At the edge of the shore, away from the group, a large eagle landed.

"Hello Winston, it's your friend Tom," he said nudging the little shell. "We heard you've been inside your shell for quite a while. We came here to check on you and see how you are doing."

Winston yawned, "I am fine inside my shell. Thank you for coming all the way from the north. Did you have difficulty finding me?"

"Oh no, not hard at all," he said. "From the north it's the other way around."

Vox snickered, "we expected to be here sooner, however, we went to the wrong south." Leo and Damian giggled. "We crashed into Big Tree Rock."

"Oh no," said Winston. "Is everyone okay?"

"More than okay," said Vox and she told the story of how they became friends with Bertie,

Damian's disappearance, and the flying hats. "You never know where you'll make a new friend."

Damian, waving his hands in the air said, "Bertie, come meet Winston and Ruby."

Bertie's wings flapped, kicking up dusty sand, as she flew the short distance towards them. Her yellow feet touched the ground as she tucked her wings to her sides. Bertie towered over everyone.

Ruby gasped and hid behind Tom.

"Hello everyone," she said while squeezing a small blue knitted cap on her head. Dripping water from the cap rolled down her face. "I'm Bertie" Lowering her beak towards Ruby, Bertie flashed a broad smile.

Ruby did not smile back.

Scooping Ruby into his arms, Tom said, "it's okay, she only eats fish."

From inside his shell, Winston's eyes grew wide with amazement.

"It's safe Ruby, go on, say hello," Tom said.

"Can we be friends?" said Bertie, her eyes sparkling with excitement.

"Any friend of Tom's is my friend too." Ruby's small paw shook Bertie's large feather. "I like your hat. Nice to meet you." Looking back at the little red turtle she said, "Winston, come meet our new friend Bertie."

Winston's head poked out just enough to have a peek. "From Big Tree Island, jeepers, nice to meet you."

"I used to wear hats to hide my bald head. Now, I love my bald head and I love hats. My friends helped me figure this out." Gesturing her wing towards Tom, Damian, and the racoons, she said, "Friends help each other." Bertie beamed, proud of her new knowledge.

"Bertie is going to be teaching Tom directions," said Vox.

Tom tried again. "You see, your friends came here to help. Won't you please come out?"

The crowd became quiet, anticipating Winston's response. Ruby wrung her hands.

Winston sighed from inside his shell. "Well, there's something I've kept secret. A strange thing about me."

The confused friends surrounding him shared glances, curious to know what he meant.

"Are you sure you will still like me?"

"Whatever it is, we are always your friends," said Tom.

"He's right," Vox said.

"It's true, friends no matter what," Leo said.

Damian with a serious expression said, "I ask too many questions and my friends don't mind. Wait—" Damian's eyes grew wide. "I have an important question growing right now."

"We are trying to help Winston, but we don't want you to burst," Tom said teasing. "Please, just ask one."

"I have so many, but there is an important question." He leaned low to see Winston's face. "Winston, everyone wants you to come out right away. What do you want to do?"

Winston's mouth dropped open and he blinked in surprise. "I, well, I have never been asked before. Let me think..."

"Good question Damian, very good question," said Tom.

Chapter 12
Oh, How Lovely

They had gathered beside Winston's log a few feet away from the shore. At Tom's feet sat the red shell of his friend Winston.

Tom sat on the sand, tired from his trip and wanting to be closer to Winston. "I'm sorry we didn't ask what you wanted sooner, well, I was just so worried, I wanted you out right away. What do you say?"

"Maybe I might—," he said. "I'm thinking possibly—"

Tom realized something. "You know, Bertie enjoys wearing hats, Damian craves answers, and I yearn a quiet sail." Perhaps Winston wished for something quite different. "It is your choice to come out of your shell or not."

The friends were quiet, watching the shell's opening to see Winston's next move. It seemed all of nature held its breath. Trees slowed their rustling and waves slackened their gurgling.

"I've decided." Winston blinked. "I am going to trust my friends and show my secret." Before his friends could respond, he continued, "but not until it is very dark outside."

"Okay Winston. It's only a few hours away, let us know when you are ready," Ruby said satisfied with the outcome.

The southern shore of Sparrow Lake came alive with music. Leo's fingers pumped the trumpet valves letting notes rise and fall in harmony with Vox's singing. As her voice rose, she strummed the cello. The cheerful melody swayed the friends to dance.

Ruby's nimble feet glided across the sandy beach shore. Damian stretched his long arms over his head and leapt into the air with a twirl. Laughter filled the air. Tom and Bertie shifted from foot to foot. Trees were swaying as if moving to the music. Winston could be heard humming from inside his red shell.

The setting sun began tipping below the tops of the trees. "Look, the North Star," said Bertie pointing into the sky. "It's the brightest star in the night sky."

Tom, glancing at Winston said, "What a pretty sky and it's a very clear night to see stars."

The sky had turned a dark purple with the fading sun. Above them the shining reflection of the moon danced on the lake.

"Yes," Winston said. "This is my favourite time, when all the stars shine down. I am ready and please don't laugh at me."

Ruby Moused clasped her hands together in front of her lips, her eyes wide with wonder. The others had gathered around, ready to learn his secret.

"These are good friends," said Bertie. "Nobody laughs at my bald head, and nobody will laugh at whatever your secret may be."

Tom said, "don't worry Winston, go on, show us."

"Okay," said Winston. "Watch what happens when I stick all my limbs outside of my shell." He paused, nervously said, "ready?"

"Ready!" his friends said.

Winston stuck out his head, then all four legs outside his shell. A yellow light rose from his shell. It grew brighter, changing to a warm orange and illuminating the air around him. The glow continued to swell, spreading across the sand and into the water.

"Well, what do you think?" said Winston.

"You are amazing!" said Tom, "What a wonderful surprise!"

Stunned, the friends stared in amazement. The warm light shone over the animals who were smiling at the little turtle.

Unable to contain herself, Ruby ran to Winston. "Oh, how lovely!" Wrapping her arms around his shell she said, "Winston, your red shell is even more marvelous! I love it!"

"How do you do it? When did you figure out how to glow?" Damian said jumping up and down. "It's so exciting!"

"One night I couldn't sleep," Winston said. "I went outside and noticed a strange light behind the long grass."

"Fireflies, right? I bet it was fireflies," said Leo.

"Nope." Winston chuckled, "I went to look. Behind the tall grass I found the most beautiful sparkling mushrooms."

"Oh no, what happened next," Vox said with whiskers twitching.

"They smelled amazing." Winston's nose rose into the air pretending to sniff.

Ruby, pressing her hands onto her forehead said, "no Winston! Mushrooms can make you sick. Please tell me you didn't eat one."

"No, I didn't eat one. I ate them all," he said, pleased with himself.

Vox groaned. "I understand," said Vox and she shrugged, "a good snack is hard to stop at just one."

Winston continued to explain. "I began walking back to the log, and by the time I got there, I was bright."

"Oh my," said Ruby shaking her head side to side. "Why didn't you tell me?"

"I know I'm not supposed to eat strange things, but mostly, I thought you'd be upset with me," said Winston, "and what if my friends think I'm odd?"

Ruby sighed and patted his shell, "oh dear, poor little Winston."

Winston cast his eyes to the sand, embarrassed and said, "I decided to just stay in, and nobody would find out what I had done."

"It might take a long time to wear off, since you ate so many," said Ruby,

"Why does it glow when he comes out and not when he is inside?" said Damian.

Ruby nodded and said, "The sparkling mushrooms have a powder that makes them twinkle. I'd guess, sticking out your limbs stirs up the powder and it oozes out of Winston's shell."

Tom said. "You know, I feel much better since Bertie offered to help me learn directions. I am curious, Winston. How do you feel now?"

A broad smile rounded the little red turtle's cheeks. "I feel great. Not just because I shared my secret, though. I am very glad my friends are here. Thanks Tom, for bringing everyone."

Tom thought, yes, Winston is right. "I think we will come south more often." The idea of sailing alone no longer felt as important. "I enjoy sailing with my friends. I can practice my directions and we can all dance on the sand."

Winston, appearing pleased with this idea and said, "I will never hide my glow again."

The End.

Dedication

In a random order, a big thanks to the people below:

Mike Clayton, for giving me space to do my art and supporting my creative process.

Keegan Simpson, for insightful input and inspiration.

My family, (parents, sister, cousins, aunts too! you know who you are),
your encouragement kept me going on this long process.

Trina Brooks, fellow author and friend, for sharing my enthusiasm.

Joan Linden, an editor with a keen eye.

Tango the cat, for not stepping on my wet drawings.

Holly the dog, (RIP) for keeping my feet warm when I was writing.

And especially, all my readers, thank you very much for cracking open my books. Writing and illustrating books brings me great pleasure. I hope you enjoy *Winston Won't Come Out*.

Diane Simpson
Writer & Illustrator

About the Author

Diane writes about animals who talk, bugs with attitudes, and imaginary places.

She lives in the small town of West Lorne and likes baking, gardening, and reading. Before writing children's books. Diane achieved a diploma in Fashion Design. Currently she works at a hospital in Medical Administration. Her love of stories and art led her to write and illustrate kids' stories.

If you join her mailing list, you'll receive a bi-monthly newsletter with updates on her book's progress, surveys on character names and contests. You can connect with Diane and scope out her latest illustrations on Facebook at:

www.facebook.com/Studio.Simpson

Her first children's book, The Mud Hill Battle, has pleased 7-year-olds across Canada. First time readers attempting to read on their own will adore her silly characters.

Questions for the Reader

- What was your favorite part of the book? Why?

- Who was your favorite character? Why?

- What was the most interesting thing you learned from the book?

- Why do you think the author wrote this book?

- Would you have ended the book differently? Did it end the way you thought it would?

- Did the problem of the book's plot get solved?

- If you could change one thing in the book, what would it be?

- Where is the book set?

- If the main character in that story lived next door, would you be friends?

- What does the place look like in your head as you read? Would you want to visit there?

Thanks for reading!

If you enjoyed this book, please leave a review on Google or Facebook.